OUTREACH

D1541049

DATE DUE

MAR 0 2 1996		
JUL 2 6 1991		MAI APR 0 8 1994
SEP 27 1996		
		MAI DEC 1 2 1996
	MAI SEP 0 7 1997	
NOV 07 1997 JAN 2 7 1998		

HELLO, SNOW!

A Grosset & Dunlap **ALL ABOARD BOOK**™

With love to my son, David J. Lewison—W.C.L.

To Anthony—Love, Auntie Maryann

ISBN 0-448-40486-9 A B C D E F G H I J

HELLO, SNOW!

By
Wendy Cheyette Lewison

Illustrated by
Maryann Cocca-Leffler

Grosset & Dunlap, Publishers

Snow! Snow! Hello, snow!
Glad to see you, don't you know?

Hello, snowsuit! Hello, hat—
Mittens, boots, and things like that.

Here's the shovel, there's the sled,
Left all summer in the shed.

All the trash cans in a row
Look like people dressed in snow.

Snow! Snow! Hello, snow!
Covering everything we know!

Covering ground that's hard and bare—
We can make snow angels there.

Shake, shake, shake the lacy trees.

Feed the hungry chickadees.

Catch some snowflakes in the air.

Slide down big hills if we dare.

Snow! Snow! Hello, snow!
Freezing cold from head to toe.
Here we come—

look out **below!**

Build a snowman, round and fat.
Give him Daddy's old felt hat.

Follow footprints, **large** and small
What strange creatures made them all?

Snow! Snow! Hello, snow!
All the cars go oh-so-slow.
(Some of them won't even go.)

Here's the snowplow with its crew.
Stand aside and let them through!

Snow! Snow! Hello, snow!
Glad to see you, don't you know?

Hope you never go away.
Just stay and stay and stay
And STAY!